PENNY & PRYCE

A SPICETOPIA STORY

PHOEBE ALEXANDER

MOUNTAINS WANTED
PUBLISHING & INDIE AUTHOR SERVICES

Cover design by the author, made with images licensed through DepositPhotos.
Paperback ISBN: 978-1-949394-58-0

Published by Mountains Wanted Publishing
P.O. Box 1014
Georgetown, DE 19947
mountainswanted.com

❀ Created with Vellum

WELCOME TO SPICETOPIA

Spicetopia Map

PART I
TWENTY YEARS AGO

PRYCE

I didn't want to go on this dumb trip. I was too old for a little kids' amusement park, so my parents let me bring my buddy Cameron along. They were so busy celebrating my little sister's birthday, they pretty much let Cameron and me do whatever we wanted.

We were bound and determined to find some fun—and probably mischief—at Sweetopia.

The park was corny, hokey, and juvenile, but there was some entertainment to be had for two teenage boys. While my sister got done up like a princess at the Sweetopia Salon, Cameron and I were banished to the pool. Two fifteen-year-old boys with no adult supervision? What could go wrong?

"Yo, check out the girl in the pink and blue bikini over there by the waterslide." Cameron waggled his dark caterpillar-esque eyebrows at me before his gaze darted back over to some lounge chairs on the other side of the pool.

It didn't take long to spot the girl he was drooling over. She was piling her long copper-colored hair into a bun on top of her head while someone—her sister, perhaps?—slathered her freckled shoulders with sunscreen.

"Holy shit, look at those tits." I elbowed my best friend in the ribs, but I couldn't tear my eyes away from her curvy figure.

Cameron let out a low whistle. "She's gotta be older than us, right? With a rack like that?"

"Only one way to find out." I sucked in a deep breath, puffed out my chest and started to march in her direction.

"Wait!" Cameron called after me, hustling to catch up. "I saw her first. You can't—"

"Can't what?" I laughed as he grabbed my arm to stop my forward motion. Not daunted in the least, I jerked it away from him and speedily zoomed toward my target.

He soon caught up, jogging right on my heels. "What're you gonna do?"

I waited until we were only a few feet from the beautiful redhead, then I whipped around to face my best friend. "Sorry, man." I smirked as I shoved him hard into the water.

He squealed like a pig as he belly-flopped into the deep end of the pool. I squared my jaw and dove in after him, pretending to make a heroic rescue as he flailed about, splashing and screaming. A lifeguard perched on his stand at the end of the pool stood up and blew his whistle at us, but by that time, I had my arm around my friend and was swimming him to the side with strong, masterful strokes.

"What the fuck was that about?" Cameron sputtered as he shook the water out of his hair like a wet dog.

"Impressing the girl, duh," I stated, looking up at the pool deck to see if she'd noticed us.

She was standing there with a less-than-impressed snarl on her face. She turned to her sister—had to be her sister because they had the same copper hair and thick, curvy build—and they both laughed.

I launched myself toward the ladder, racing up the steps so I could go over and talk to her, but by the time I reached her, she and her sister had joined the queue for the waterslide. Wasting no time, I grabbed Cameron, and we booked it toward the line while the lifeguard continued to glare at us from across the pool.

By the time we got there, twenty people or so had filled in the space behind the girl in the blue and pink bikini and her sister.

"Tough luck," Cameron said with a shrug. "She was supposed to be mine anyway."

PENNY

Piper dragged me into the line for the roller coaster right behind Kyle and Liam. She'd been hot on Kyle's heels all day, and I was getting tired of being the third wheel. I knew she was trying to get me interested in Liam, but just no. He smelled like a giant sweaty armpit and only seemed to know one-syllable words.

I should have gone with our parents today instead of hanging out with my older sister. It was my younger brother's first time at Sweetopia, and they were taking him on all the kiddie rides. So it was either that or hang with Piper, her crush and his best friend.

We went to Sweetopia every summer over the Fourth of July, and every year it got worse.

I was too old for princesses, and I practically got cavities from walking down the sweets-themed streets. Plus, I wasn't a roller coaster person. At all.

This line wasn't even moving. Maybe I'd gotten lucky, and the ride had broken down.

Nah, I never got lucky.

I tapped my sister's shoulder, interrupting her conversation with Kyle. "Piper, I need to use the restroom."

When she whipped around to face me, there was a vicious glare in her turquoise eyes. "You can go after the ride. It's only like two minutes long, Penny. I'm sure you can hold it."

My nostrils flared as my hands flew to my hips. "But we've been in line for twenty minutes, and it's not even moving."

Just then, the people in the row next to us started to move. A wide space opened up, and the people in front of us filled it, and then we followed, and it continued like a wave through the entire queue. I trudged forward, grateful we were finally moving when, suddenly, someone rammed right into me.

"Hey!" I snarled, turning around to glare at the imbecile who dared to annoy me. Recognition instantly dawned. It was the two idiotic boys who were showing off in the pool yesterday. The blond one pushed the dark-haired one in and pretended to rescue him.

"Watch where you're going!" I snapped at them.

"Sorry." The blond one grinned at me, not looking the least bit sorry. His buddy elbowed him in the ribs, and they both snickered.

I was usually pretty easy-going, but with my red hair came the legendary ginger temper—and the beast had already been poked by Piper and her stupid friends. "What is your problem?" I snarked in the boys' general direction.

"My friend thinks you're hot," the dark-haired boy piped up. The blond immediately punched him in the arm.

The line moved again, so I turned to face the front, giving myself time to think and potentially wish away the blush that had spread across my cheeks. I'd wondered yesterday if they were showing off to get my attention, but I assumed they were interested in Piper, not me. She was older and slimmer. Boys were drawn to her like moths to a flame. I was shorter, fatter. I did have bigger boobs though, so I had that going for me.

We stopped again, and I could feel their stares burning holes into my back. Then there was a tap on my shoulder.

"Hey, I'm sorry for ramming into you," the blond said with a soft twangy accent. "I'm Pryce, by the way. We saw you at the pool yesterday."

I spun around again. "Oh? I didn't notice you," I lied.

My cheeks flushed again. *Damn it.*

The line kept moving forward. We were getting closer to boarding. I watched the platform ahead as the train of cars, shaped and painted to look like hard candies, zoomed in, jerking to a stop at a control panel, where a park employee in a candy-striped uniform was waiting for one group of riders to disembark and another to board before they rocketed off the platform and through a dark tunnel.

My heart raced. Butterflies did the fox trot in my stomach when I noticed each row had three seats.

Three!

There were four of us.

Kyle, Liam, Piper and me.

So now what?

I looked back at the blond who had been trying to chat me up, the one whose friend claimed he thought I was hot. There were two of them, and one of me.

Did that mean I would ride with them?

"You okay, Red?" the dark-haired guy asked, his thick brows furrowing as his eyes raked up and down my body. "I'm Cameron, by the way. I wasn't really drowning yesterday when this dumbass jumped in and pretended to save me. I can totally swim. I'm a great swimmer, in fact."

I suppressed a giggle. They were both kind of cute, but Pryce...he had these chocolate-brown eyes that didn't seem to go with his blond hair. They were intriguing. They tilted up at the corners, matching the slant of his prominent cheekbones and his sharply cut jaw. His hair was on the longer side, and he kept running his fingers through it. His skin was so tan, it was nearly bronze. And his arms were bigger around than mine.

Which was saying something because mine were pretty thick.

I hadn't noticed that yesterday, probably because my sister said they were stupid immature boys, and we should ignore them. *I should make it a point not to listen to her*, I chided myself.

"How old are you guys?" I blurted out.

Cameron puffed out his chest. "I'm fifteen. You?"

"I'm fifteen and a half," Pryce added. His slow drawl did things to my insides.

I giggled. "I'm fourteen and a half."

I didn't miss the way Pryce's dark eyes bugged out. They probably thought I was older than them, not younger. Most people did—it was the boobs. Sometimes people thought I was the older sister, even though Piper was taller. She was seventeen.

Maybe riding the roller coaster with them wouldn't be half bad.

PRYCE

When we first got into the line for this coaster, all I could think about was how long the wait would be. Now, standing here with this gorgeous redhead with big tits and the most amazing eyes that looked like the ocean, I couldn't believe the wait was almost over.

I wanted to start the line all over again just to have more time to talk to her.

"You never told us your name," I blurted out.

"It's Penelope," she said. "Penny for short."

Penny. Of course. Her hair was exactly the same color as a penny. It was the perfect name for the perfect girl. Suddenly Sweetopia had gotten a whole lot sweeter.

Penny's sister turned around, grabbed her wrist and jerked her over to the side. Standing so close, it was impossible not to eavesdrop.

"You can ride with Liam, and I'll ride with Kyle," the sister said in a bossy tone.

"It's three people in a row," Penny snapped back.

Ahead, the candy-striped park workers were grouping people by threes and having them stand in front of wooden gates, one for each car. They weren't allowing single riders or even two riders to queue up in front of a gate.

And then: "Groups of three. Get in your group of three before you reach the front of the line, or we'll put you in groups," he announced in a vaguely threatening way. His expression told me he was thoroughly peopled out for the day.

The sister groaned, her nostrils flaring. She glanced back at the boys she was with, who were both bigger than Cameron and me, probably rising seniors, if I had to guess. We were sophomores.

"She's riding with us." I stepped forward, giving her sister a confident smirk and crossing my arms over my chest so she knew I meant business.

"Whatever." She rolled her eyes.

Penny's beautiful, luscious lips spread into a smile. "Thank you. I did not want to ride with them," she admitted.

Next thing I knew, we were being directed to our gate. When our cars arrived, Cameron and I did the chivalrous thing and let Penny sit between us. She leaned over and whispered in my ear, "Sorry in advance if I scream. I hate roller coasters."

"You do? Then why are you—"

I shouldn't question fate. Duh.

"My sister didn't give me a choice. My parents said I had to stay with her at all times." She sighed.

"It's okay. I'll take care of you," I promised, flashing her my most charming smile.

"I'm sure I'll be fine. I just might scream." She shrugged. "That's why I'm warning you."

The car jerked forward. The worker in the control booth signaled his colleagues who were checking the lap bars to make sure they were locked. They exchanged thumbs-up, and, with no further warning, we shot off like a rocket into a black tunnel with pink and white lights, twisting and turning until we exited the other side and slowly cranked up a hill.

Sweetopia lay spread before us, the people looking like tiny ants at such a great height. We slowly lurched forward until we tipped over the edge, soaring down the hill so fast, I thought we might fly off the tracks. It was exhilarating.

And not just the roller coaster.

The scream that pierced my eardrum faded away as a small, warm hand clutched mine and didn't let go.

Even when we jerked to a stop at the platform approximately two minutes later.

2

PENNY

*a*fter spending the rest of the day in the park together, that night after we ate dinner with our respective families, Pryce and I met up at the pool. My sister and her friends were on the other side of the sprawling complex, distracted and not paying attention to us, and I wasn't sure where Cameron was. My little brother was so exhausted from his day at the theme park that my parents decided to stay up in the room with him. Judging by how they looked at dinner, I was pretty sure they were just as exhausted as he was.

Behind the waterslide was a grotto concealed by a waterfall that, at night, was lit with pink, purple and turquoise lights. I was wearing my neon green tankini with the zipper on the top half. Pryce wore navy swim trunks with little palm trees and sharks on them. The sun had sunk low in the sky, and twilight had painted the clouds in tranquil shades of dusky mauve and smoky blue.

Pryce was splashing around and showing off when I grabbed him by the arm and pulled him into the deeper part of the pool in the grotto. He grinned, realizing we were alone on this side, and the waterfall was blocking us from everyone's view. "Can you tread water?" he asked, concern edging his voice.

"Of course I can." I scoffed at him. "Even if I couldn't, I'm pretty buoyant." I looked down at my chest and laughed.

His attention was drawn to the zipper, which was all the way up. "That thing is teasing me," he admitted, shaking his head and chuckling.

"Oh, yeah?" I shot back. My legs kicked smoothly under the water, keeping me afloat as I jerked the zipper down, exposing my ample cleavage. Most girls my age weren't as blessed in the boobage department as I was, and I could practically see the drool forming in Pryce's mouth as his honey-brown eyes widened and he took in the view.

"Holy shit," he managed, the words coming out with a puff of a breath. He started to slip beneath the surface like he momentarily forgot he needed to tread water or he'd sink.

When he sputtered a bit at the water that had seeped into his mouth, I giggled. "Well, don't drown, geez. Are you sure you can tread water?" I teased him.

Two powerful strokes took him to the side of the pool. He curled his finger and beckoned me closer. "Swim over here, okay?" He clung to the side, catching his breath.

"You're about to make me lose my mind, ya know," he said in his Texas twang.

As gracefully as possible, I closed the distance between us, joining him on the wall. "Is that so?" I lowered my eyes to his chest and bit my lip—I was pretty sure I'd read somewhere that drove boys crazy.

"I really want to kiss you," he breathed out. It was barely more than a whisper, but I was close enough to hear even with the waterfall roaring around us.

My chest heaved as I looked at him, words trapped in my throat. When I gave him the subtlest of nods, he reached out and cupped my face with one hand and angled his head as he leaned toward me.

The cool water swirled around us as his lips crashed against mine, a little too forcefully at first, and when I grunted in surprise, he tightened his grip on my jaw. His tongue darted out, suddenly soft and gentle, licking the seam and begging me to part my lips for him.

My lungs squeezed in my chest, and my heart nearly burst as he explored my mouth while his other hand dove down to caress my exposed breasts. Deepening our kiss, he pulled me flush against his body, and I could feel him pressing into me. My mind raced with so many thoughts, while my body tingled with awareness. It was sensory overload with the waterfall pounding into the water, waves lapping against our skin, colored lights flashing, and upbeat pop music flowing out of the speakers built into the rocks around us.

When I finally got my brain to work again and reluctantly pulled away to make sure we weren't being watched, Pryce's eyes were still closed, his lashes dark and wet against his tan skin. They slowly fluttered open as he sucked in a sharp breath. "Wow…" was all he could say.

Two days into this trip, I'd been ready to go home. My sister and her friends were obnoxious, and all my parents cared about was making sure our brother got to do all the stuff geared toward preschoolers.

But then I met Pryce, and I never wanted to leave.

Three days with him, and I knew it was love.

As I was standing by our pile of suitcases lined up on the curb, ready to be loaded into our minivan, I heard my name from the walkway to the building where we had been staying all week. Goosebumps pricked my skin when I recognized the voice.

My mother shot me a look that clearly communicated I needed to get my butt in the van ASAP. I smirked at her and headed over to find Pryce. He'd ducked in between a thick green bush and a pillar that supported the veranda over the patio.

We'd spent the last three days together, and it was magical. I didn't think this trip would have one moment of magic for me, but I was wrong. So wrong.

Last night we'd spent hours making out in a little gazebo we found on the other side of the tennis courts, and the tingles I felt made an encore performance as Pryce took my hand into his and wrapped my fingers around a tiny box.

"What's this?" I looked up into his dark eyes.

He smiled, his eyes crinkling and making his sharp

cheekbones even more prominent. "Just a little something to remember me by."

A little giggle bounced up my throat. "Well, there's no way I could forget you...not with you being my first kiss and all."

He was shifting from foot to foot, clearly anxious for me to open my present. "C'mon, see what it is," he urged me.

I opened the box to reveal a silver chain with a tiny castle pendant. It looked like the Cotton Candy Castle, the centerpiece of Sweetopia. The tallest tower sparkled with a pink gemstone. A thrill rushed through me. "This is beautiful, Pryce!"

"Do you want me to put it on you?" His voice trembled.

I nodded, carefully lifting the necklace from its velvet nest. He took a deep breath as if to gather his concentration and took it from me. I lifted my hair off my neck and turned around so he could see where he was clasping it.

He leaned down, his hot breath tickling my nape and sending a chill down my spine. He was so gentle as he fastened it and laid the chain to rest against my skin.

I turned around to see his eyes had turned glassy. Mine followed suit. "It looks beautiful on you," he assured me. "I'm going to miss you so much, Penny."

Tears welled up with a painful sting as I threw my arms around his neck and buried my face in his chest. "I'm going to miss you too." He squeezed me tightly to his body.

He lived in Texas, and I lived in Maryland. When you're fourteen and fifteen, you might as well be on different planets. I didn't quite grasp it then, but, looking back now, it was doubtful we'd ever see each other again.

We had exchanged addresses though. And we promised to be pen pals.

My mother's voice carried on the wind in that shrill way I hated, "Penelope Marie Taylor, it's time to go!" Every time she spoke to me, it spawned an involuntary eyeroll.

I broke our embrace and yelled back at her, "I'll be right there, geez!"

"Guess you have to go." Pryce's lips curled down. He took my hands into his. "Can I kiss you goodbye?"

Any words I might have wanted to say in parting were stuck in my throat, so I just nodded, hoping the tears filling my eyes would stay there instead of streaking down my cheeks. I could only imagine what my sister would say if she caught me crying over this boy. She'd already teased me mercilessly about him for three days now.

I closed my eyes and let his lips brush against mine, so softly, so tenderly, until they parted and his tongue tentatively slipped inside. His arms wrapped around me again, squeezing me to his body.

For a moment, the world stopped. We were just two teenagers who'd met, shared a first kiss, and were forced to say goodbye in the heartbreakingly short span of three days.

They should rename this place Bittersweetopia.

When my eyes opened, he was gone.

PART II
PRESENT DAY

3

PENNY

"*I* can't believe I'm actually at Spicetopia!" I exclaimed, twirling in a circle on Main Street as Ben and Yvonne looked on, smiling.

Yvonne took out her phone and snapped a picture. "I haven't seen you this happy in a long time! See, I told you this trip would be good for you."

Ben leaned down and pressed a kiss to my cheek, his soft brown beard brushing against my skin. "You deserve this, babe, and so much more. I can't wait to show you all the rides and other stuff."

"Other stuff?" I shot him a devious grin. "And what exactly does this 'other stuff' entail?"

"Only the dirtiest, naughtiest, kinkiest stuff you can think of," Yvonne gushed. She grabbed my hand and pulled me inside a bar designed to look like a garage. The neon sign hanging over the sleek chrome counter glowed with the words "Lube Express."

Ben stepped right up to the bar and ordered three cocktails, something called "Greased Lightning." The femme bartender, who had shockingly pink hair and was wearing a purple leather vest that created a stunning amount of cleavage, grinned as she got to work mixing our drinks.

"This place is incredible." I took in the auto-themed décor. Everything was chrome, neon and vinyl with black-and-white checkered accents. Some of the tables looked like classic cars, and you could sit inside them. I gestured toward a pink Cadillac. "That's where I want to sit!"

Ben tipped the bartender, balanced the tray holding three neon-green concoctions, then followed us over to the Cadillac booth. Yvonne slid in next me, her bare, bronzed thigh pressing against mine. We were both wearing the tiniest of shorts, and the contrast of her dark skin against my pale was vivid and striking.

"I guess I shouldn't be surprised that it's this over the top." I took a sip of my Greased Lightning. "We visited Sweetopia every year when I was a kid. Cy Sweet must have learned to dream big from his parents' amusement park."

"Oh, yeah, Sweetopia—I've heard of that place. It was in Florida, but it's been shut down a while, right?" Yvonne leaned in, her volume rising over the music. "I heard there was some big strike over wages and benefits. I remember seeing it all over the news a few years ago."

I nodded. "Yeah, I followed that story closely since we

used to vacation there. The park was pretty cool when I was little."

"Pretty cool" was an understatement. I loved visiting Sweetopia with my family. Our last trip started off slow— I was really too old for it at that point—but then I met someone. A boy. We had a fling, and it was one of my best memories growing up. I had my first kiss there—I had a *lot* of firsts there! Whatever happened to that guy?

Leaning his stocky frame back in the Cadillac booth, Ben scanned the map on his cell phone. "So, what do you guys want to hit first? The thing I love about this place is they don't let too many people in, so the lines and waits are never that long."

"I should hope not as much as tickets cost!" Yvonne scoffed. She was already halfway through her cocktail, and we had pre-gamed back at our room. She was about to get wild, and I was here for it. It was impossible not to have fun when you were with Yvonne. She was the human form of a happy pill.

Ben and Yvonne insisted on bringing me here after my precious pup Marlon crossed over the Rainbow Bridge. I'd been moping around for a good month, and then they surprised me with this trip to the Bahamas and, specifically, a visit to Spicetopia, a new adult theme park owned by Cy Sweet, one of the heirs to the Sweetopia fortune. They'd promised to show me a good time—as long as I would consider moving in with them and becoming an exclusive throuple.

"No pressure," Ben assured me when they invited me on the trip. "We mainly just want you to have fun and get a break from teaching. You deserve it. But no pressure on the throuple thing."

"Well, maybe an itsy-bitsy teeny-weeny bit of pressure," Yvonne had joked, her fingers set in the universal symbol for a tiny amount.

I'd been dating Ben and Yvonne for about six months. They were so thrilled they'd finally found their unicorn, and they were the nicest, most loving and open couple ever. Every minute I spent with them, I was pampered and spoiled. They treated me like a precious gem. Being a teacher, that was definitely not a feeling I was accustomed to.

But I wasn't one hundred percent sold on moving in with them.

On committing to them.

Which is what they wanted.

But perhaps this week in the Bahamas would help me see us together as a family. As a throuple. I'd never been part of a throuple before. I dated mostly men through college, not really embracing my bisexual side until I was in my mid-twenties. Now I was approaching thirty-five, and I'd had a few relationships with women.

I just hadn't found The One.

But maybe that was because I was meant to find The Two—not The One?

"Why don't we check out the Virtual Fantasy pavilion after this?" Yvonne suggested. She was a big-time gamer, so it didn't surprise me she was drawn to that attraction.

"Only if we can do the Wheel of Orgasms after that!" I laughed, glancing down at the map on Ben's phone. There were so many cool attractions, it was hard to decide.

"Time is going to fly this week," Yvonne said as though she was reading my mind. "Are you both ready for this epic adventure?"

That was another thing I loved about her. She was fearless, and she really knew how to pump others up. It was no surprise she was a kindergarten teacher—a kindergarten teacher with a wild side.

That was how I met her, in fact. I taught across the hall from her. It was probably hard for most people to imagine two kindergarten teachers getting their freak on at a place like Spicetopia, but here we were!

"Penny, you finished with your drink?" Ben eyed the glass in front of me, which only had some crushed ice at the bottom. I'd even eaten the pineapple and cherry garnish.

"Yep, maybe one more for the road?"

He grinned. "Coming right up!"

"I'M NOT REALLY a roller coaster person," I protested when we came to the Flying Dildo Coaster's entrance.

"This one is pretty tame," Yvonne argued. "I don't mind riding alone if you want to ride with Ben."

I looked up at the towering metal structure as the cars whizzed by in a blur. I only discovered their phallic shape when the next train slowly climbed to the peak of the first big hill. Just thinking about how that drop would make my stomach feel was enough to give me cold feet.

"I'd really rather not," I insisted, looking up at the track again. She said it was "pretty tame," but there was a corkscrew! That didn't seem tame to me.

"Are you sure? I can stay down here with you if you don't want to ride," Ben offered.

"No, no," I waved them toward the entrance, "you two go ahead. I don't mind staying down here and people watching." There were dozens of folks walking past—literal eye candy. Some were dressed up; most were wearing revealing clothing. Several folks wore swimsuits since there was a beach and water park on property, and others rocked BDSM or fetish gear. I'd never seen such diversity, and the entire scene screamed "freedom" to me. People free to be who and what they were, with no shame, and no inhibitions.

"If you're absolutely positive." Yvonne leaned down and stroked her fingers through my copper-colored hair, which I'd left down. The soft Bahamian breeze gently blew it around my shoulders.

I grinned and nodded, then pressed a soft kiss to her cheek. "Absolutely. You two enjoy yourselves."

Ben smiled at his wife and offered her his arm. They entered the queue, heading toward the platform where they would board their own giant dildo and zip around the track. Maybe I could catch a picture of them flying down the big hill?

I'd had two of those Greased Lightning drinks and a couple of Pink Ladies shots. We passed by the entrance to the water park, but we decided we'd rather do that and the nude beach during the day and before drinking too much.

Me on a nude beach! Could I be that brave?

Observing the variety of shapes and sizes of my fellow Spicetopia visitors made me feel brave. Adding to the diversity, I saw a veritable rainbow of skin colors represented, which was amazing. I was a voluptuous size eighteen, with 40DDD tits and thick thighs, but I seemed to fit right in.

Everyone fit in, in fact, because everyone was wildly unique—and our differences were openly celebrated. It was so refreshing!

No matter what ended up happening in my relationship with Ben and Yvonne, I would always credit them with helping me learn to love myself, including my plus-size body. Bringing me to a place like this, where everyone was so uninhibited and unabashedly flaunting everything they had, it made me realize just how far I'd come. Even I was rocking a crop top and tiny shorts that rode up on my curvy ass—and I didn't feel the least bit self-conscious about it. I'd already had tons of approving glances and smiles.

Spicetopia is so welcoming, I wish could just stay here. Hmmm...I wonder if they have any elementary schools around here...

4

PRYCE

"So, what do you think?" My buddy Evan gestured to the island as the ferry made its approach. The sun was setting, silhouetting the palm trees at the entrance gates against bands of fiery scarlet and orange. And jutting up into the sky was a huge castle with a dizzying array of turrets and towers. Architecturally speaking, it was ambitious. Lots of angles and a cacophony of colors certainly provided visual interest.

But I was still skeptical. "So Cy Sweet built this with the money he and his family made at Sweetopia?" I grabbed the railing as the ferry bounced against the dock.

"Would you quit bringing up the business side of it? Geez, we're here to have fun, Pryce. Not to analyze the architectural influences or try to determine how much revenue this place is bringing in. Or what the overhead might be." Evan rolled his eyes as he gestured for me to exit the ferry ahead of him.

"Well, I enjoy those things," I reminded him with an indignant scoff. I was glad I hadn't mentioned my architectural analysis to him. I needed to see the other buildings first.

"You're so damn serious all the time! No wonder Dana left you." He huffed in exasperation as we climbed down to the dock, then made our way to the Spicetopia entrance, which was all lit up in multicolored lights.

I sighed. "I already told you this trip is dumb. Who goes on a trip to celebrate a divorce? It's a terrible fiscal—"

"Shut up! If I hear 'fiscal' or 'ROI' or anything of that ilk come out of your mouth in the next three days, I swear to god, I'm going to cover you in chum and throw you overboard." Evan chuckled at his colorful threat. "If you can't have fun at Spicetopia, you're hopeless, you know that?"

"Yeah, well, I'm not *celebrating* my divorce. I just want to get laid and move on with my life. Then, when I get back to Houston, I can start focusing on finding someone to start a family with."

"There you go, trying to plan everything out again. Could you just relax and try to put your life plan on hold for three fucking days, bro?" He pushed me toward the gate, where we had to scan our rings that gave us access to the theme park, our hotel room, and any other amenities we wished to enjoy during our stay. "As soon as we get inside, we're finding the nearest bar and getting you liquored up. Surely that will loosen you up a bit. For fuck's sake, Pryce. Live a little!"

"Fine. Whatever you want to do." I sighed as I scanned my ring and was greeted by a busty blonde Spicetopia employee.

I'd always had a preference for redheads, but a blonde would do. Or a brunette. I wasn't in a position to be picky when I just needed to get my head screwed on right again.

Dana had turned my world upside down, and now I had to find my footing again. How could she decide three years into marriage that she didn't want kids? Worse yet, she insisted she'd never wanted them and that I'd been perfectly aware of that fact when we tied the knot.

I was thirty-six years old—I wasn't getting any younger. I thought for sure I'd have a couple of rugrats by the time I was forty, but it was looking less and less likely. I'd always wanted kids, since I was a kid myself.

I'd find my footing as soon as I fucked my way out of this depression I'd been in ever since I signed the divorce papers. Yes, Evan was right. I needed to relax and let my libido lead the way at Spicetopia…

EVAN and I ended up at the Hidden Treasures Casino, and I even made a little extra cash playing blackjack. Next we hit The Scream House, a dark ride with a macabre collection of gruesome scenes, and we checked out the towering and exquisitely detailed Rainbow Castle. As an architect, I found the structure and layout fascinating— could probably spend all day picking the architect's brain.

We made a reservation at the Fantasies Fulfilled restaurant at the top of the castle for dinner tomorrow night.

Then we hopped aboard the Mythical Beasts Carousel —I rode the dragon—and it was relaxing, but, after that, we were both ready for something a little more heart-pumping. "So…how are you supposed to meet chicks here?" I asked Evan as we walked down the palm-lined path toward the next attraction.

"There are several meet and greets," he answered. "We just haven't been at the right place at the right time yet. I figured we'd experience the rides tonight and focus on getting some action tomorrow night."

I loved roller coasters and rides as much as anyone, but I was hoping to be sinking into a tight, wet pussy tonight. It was already nine o'clock, the sun had set, and I hadn't even met one woman yet. Sure, I'd waved or said hello to a few ladies who were in line near us, but no numbers were exchanged or anything. The website made it sound like we'd have hordes of sexy ladies all clamoring for our cocks. False advertising, maybe?

"Oh, damn." Evan's head tilted slightly toward a pair of bronze-skinned beauties with waist-length dark hair. "Think they're sisters?"

The mention of "sisters" took me right back to my last trip to Sweetopia. I'd been thinking about it a lot since we were in basically the adult version of the kiddie park my family frequented when I was growing up. I'd met a pair of sisters there, and the younger sister and I had a three-day fling. When I closed my eyes, I could even see her, the memories painted vividly on the canvas of my mind.

I looked over to where my buddy had gestured. Not

exactly my type, but I couldn't deny they were hot as fuck. "Yeah, maybe, why, you want to go say hi?"

"After the roller coaster," Evan said, looking up past the tree line.

We came to a clearing, and above the trees, I saw a twisting metal track with cars zooming by. "Holy shit, are those—"

"Yep, those are giant dildos, my friend." Evan was beaming. Clearly, he wanted a ride. "C'mon, the wait's not too long right now."

I cocked my head. "So, no sisters for us?"

"Look, I think they're getting in line too." He smirked as the girls tossed the drinks they'd been sipping and made their way toward the queue. His eyebrows waggled as he gestured for me to go first.

I rushed toward the end of the line so we could be next to the bronze beauties, but when I whipped back around to say something to Evan, a bright flash of copper caught my eye at a railing farther down the sidewalk. It looked to be the ride exit.

"What are you looking at, man?" Evan peered in the same direction, trying to figure out what had captured my attention.

"Just a sec," I held up one finger, "I'll be right back."

Evan rolled his eyes. He didn't like it when I deviated from the plan—which I understood because I didn't like to deviate from the plan either. That was one of the main reasons he and I got along so well. It was just that my plans were usually of a professional nature, and his were generally of a social nature.

I snaked through the line that had gathered since we

joined the queue. When I looked over at the spot where I thought I saw someone I knew, no one was there. I blinked a few times, wondering if I'd just imagined it because I was thinking about her only a few minutes ago.

Right. That trip to Sweetopia was over twenty years ago.

I didn't even know what she looked like now. Maybe she wasn't a redhead anymore?

And she probably wouldn't even remember me anyway.

I turned around, thinking I should head back to the Flying Dildo line to find Evan when a flash of copper caught my eye again. A tall, curvy redhead was walking away from a food cart holding a snow cone, her pink tongue darting out to lick the turquoise flavoring on top.

Penny? It couldn't be, right?

I rushed toward her, following her to the spot at the railing she'd occupied moments before. As I got closer to her, taking in her beautiful voluptuous figure, long legs and flaming tresses, the less confident I was that it was actually *my* Penny. She was even more beautiful than I remembered—downright breathtaking, in fact.

Well, what have you got to lose? I asked myself. *She may not be Penny, but she is definitely your type, and didn't you want to meet someone anyway?*

Her blue eyes blinked as she lifted her head, focusing on me. Her auburn brows drew together, but nothing resembling recognition flashed across her face.

"Hi." I smiled.

"Um, hi." She licked the snow cone again and then crunched down on the ice.

33

"Is this your first time visiting Spicetopia?" I asked as her eyes darted back to mine.

She looked flustered, a blush spreading across her creamy white cheeks. "Uh, yeah... Yours too?"

"You don't remember me, do you?" Was it her? I couldn't tell, but something drew me to her.

"What?" Her brows pulled together again as two figures approached her from behind, a man and a woman. The woman slung her arms around Penny's waist and squeezed her.

"Oh my god, that was so awesome!" the woman exclaimed. "I can't believe you missed out!"

She whipped around to face the couple, never answering my question. The short, squat, bearded man pulled her close to his body with the toned, athletic woman still attached on the other side, making a Penny sandwich—if it was, in fact, Penny. I was starting to doubt it.

I was just about to walk away when I heard the man say: "Okay, that was fun. Penny, you should pick the next ride."

5

PENNY

I was staring at this stranger who came up to me while I was waiting for Ben and Yvonne to get off the coaster. Something about him was familiar, but I couldn't figure out what.

He said something like, "You don't remember me?" but, before I could respond, I was ambushed by my partners. Yvonne slung her arms around my waist, and Ben hugged me tight to his body, almost protectively, like he was afraid this man was hitting on me.

"Okay, that was fun. Penny, you should pick the next ride!" Ben exclaimed, pulling me away from the man, who was still looking at me with dark eyes and bronze skin. He was wearing a hat, so I couldn't see his hair, but those eyes, those sharp cheekbones...they did trigger something...

And then it clicked.

Pryce.

Sweetopia.

My first kiss.

No, it couldn't be him. Could it?

When I turned back, he was gone.

MY FEET ACHED by the time we made it back to our room. The accommodations were lovely, everything upscale and luxurious. We had a king-sized bed and a spacious bathroom. Ben and Yvonne showered together, and then I took my turn.

The bathroom was still steamy, so I left the door open while I ran water for a bath. I felt like soaking my tired feet, and there was a swanky-looking collection of Spicetopia-branded toiletries, including bubble bath. As the water filled the giant round jacuzzi tub, I stood at the vanity looking through the travel-sized jewelry box I'd brought, pulling out a necklace. A tiny silver castle with a pink gemstone dangled from the chain.

I'd had it since the last day I was ever at Sweetopia. I wore it for years—every day, in fact—until my senior year of college when it was starting to look a little tarnished. Then I put it in my jewelry box, and it had been there ever since. For some reason—nostalgia, most likely—I transferred it into this travel-sized box when I packed for this trip.

I was fourteen and a half years old that summer, and Pryce and I spent three glorious days making out like horny teenagers—well, we *were* horny teenagers, after all.

We didn't go *all the way*, but he was the first person to give me an orgasm. I received the necklace the day my family left Sweetopia to go back home to Maryland. He said he gave it to me hoping I'd never forget him.

I hadn't.

Just thinking of that night we'd gone behind the waterfall and grotto at the Sweetopia pool sent tingles down my spine. I could smell the chlorine in his hair, the scent of cotton candy lingering around us—it seemed to be piped in at Sweetopia. The feel of his nimble fingers as they explored every inch of my body. The sounds of his soft breath falling against my skin and his Texas twang as he told me what he wanted to do to me.

I'd spent almost every night of my adolescence pondering what it would have been like to give myself to him, to make love with him—among other questions, like, did he ever think about me?

We exchanged a couple of letters—this was before most kids had cell phones and before there was such a thing as social media. By Christmas that year, I had a boyfriend—Jacob. I still wore the Cotton Candy Castle necklace though.

Then, after college, I didn't think of Pryce hardly ever, but, now and again, a vivid memory would suddenly pop into my head. It always brought a smile to my face, and I wondered what happened to him. Where he was. What he was doing. If he had ever found The One.

Surely that man staring at me as I licked my snow cone outside the Flying Dildo Coaster was *not* Pryce. Shit, I couldn't even remember his last name now. In my mind, he seemed to be more of a legend than a real person.

"Everything okay?" Yvonne's voice snapped me out of my reverie as she gingerly stepped into the still steamy bathroom.

"Yeah, I'm fine, just filling up the tub." I smiled at her as she made her way over to me.

"What's that?" She pointed to my hand, which was still holding the necklace.

"Oh…" I looked down at the tiny pendant and smiled. "So…you're going to think this is weird."

She reached out and stroked a finger down my cheek. "Try me?"

I hesitated, not sure I wanted to share my memories of Pryce. I'd never told anyone about him, in fact. Well, my sister knew, but she teased me so much about him, I never mentioned his name again after we left Sweetopia.

If I didn't have the gift he gave me the day we said goodbye, I might have worried I just made him up. Telling someone seemed to take some of the magic away.

"Come on, beautiful. I know you have something going on in that big, brilliant mind of yours." Yvonne grasped my face in her palms and leaned in, brushing her full, luscious lips against mine. An electric shock coursed through me. She always knew how to push my buttons.

"Okay, fine, you'll think I'm crazy, but whatever." I took a deep breath, and she pulled back to look at me, curiosity shining in her chocolate-brown eyes. "So, when I was a kid, we went on family vacations to Sweetopia—"

Her head tilted, brown corkscrew curls dangling to the side of her dark skin. "Yeah, you mentioned that earlier."

"The last time we visited there, I was fourteen. We were really there for my little brother, and my sister and I were basically left to our own devices. Naturally, I met a boy..."

Yvonne's eyes widened, and she clapped her hands together. "A boy! Sounds romantic!"

I gave a wistful sigh. "It was. I've probably made it out to be so much better in my mind than it actually was, but he was my first kiss, and he gave me this necklace when we parted ways. But I never saw him again... He lived in Texas."

"Aww, what a sweet story—pardon the pun." She waggled her brows at me. "Let me see it?" She reached out her hand, and I placed the necklace in her open palm. She studied it, a smile spreading across her full lips. "So cute. I bet you wore it all the time, didn't you?"

I nodded. "I know it's crazy, but...tonight when I was waiting for you and Ben to come off the roller coaster, I thought I saw him. But it was probably my imagination."

She blinked twice. "You thought you saw the boy from Sweetopia—your first kiss?"

I nodded. "Silly, right?"

She practically sang, "Oh, my stars, that would be so amazing! Maybe you'll run into him again. Why didn't you talk to him?"

"I'm sure it wasn't really him," I argued. "Sometimes I feel like I made the whole thing up, you know? It was so long ago, and I was so young. I should call my sister and see if she remembers him—"

"If you did find him here, what would you want to do with him?" She blinked a few more times.

I stared at her. I wasn't in a monogamous relationship with Ben and Yvonne, but that was what they wanted.

That was why they'd brought me on this trip. They wanted me to see how wonderful it would be to be part of a throuple with them. In the meantime, I was free to explore and have other partners.

So, could I admit to her I wanted to kiss Pryce again? His lips were so soft… I needed to know if they were as soft as I remembered them being.

"I'm not sure," I lied, then laughed to cover it up, giving a little shrug. "I'm sure it's all a figment of my overactive imagination and too many Greased Lightnings!"

"And on that note," she said, "I think you better get in that tub before it overflows, and then come to bed. We're exhausted! Tomorrow is going to be so much fun. We better get some rest first though."

Nodding, I reached over to turn off the faucet. "Okay. I'll be there soon."

She wrapped her arms around my waist and pulled me in for another kiss. "Goodnight, beautiful."

"So, Kink Link…you guys in?" Ben looked up from his phone, his eyes darting between me and Yvonne.

"And what kink do you want to explore, my love?" Yvonne questioned as she dabbed perfume on her pulse points. She was wearing a tiny pair of white shorts and a fuchsia tube top that didn't leave much to the imagination. Her bronze skin glowed with the glittery lotion she'd applied earlier.

I had chosen a bubblegum-pink babydoll dress with lace around the edges that accentuated my abundant curves and showcased my ample bosom in all its glory. *Who says redheads can't wear pink? Those people can kiss my voluptuous ass.*

"Well, I wouldn't mind playing exhibitionist," he waggled his eyebrows at both of us, "but I also wouldn't mind playing voyeur. I'm still pretty sore from yesterday. Guess I should have gotten in better shape before we came, huh?" He patted his thick midsection. He had somewhat of a dad bod but without the *being a father* part. He'd played football in college, though, and still had big muscles under the fluff that made my mouth water.

"I think Penny should play exhibitionist, and we should play voyeur," Yvonne suggested. She came up behind me and raked her fingers through my long copper-colored hair that almost reached my waist. "I'd love to see her get spanked by a Dom, wouldn't you, babe?"

A shiver raced up my spine. Hmm, I did find that idea somewhat intriguing.

I looked up at Ben, seeking his opinion on the matter. "If that's what you want, I will share you, Princess—" Princess Penny was his pet name for me, "—as long as you come home with us tonight. What do you say? I'm not sure I have the stamina to keep up with both of you nymphs today."

Yvonne laughed. "I'm not sure you have the stamina to keep up with *one* of us nymphs today!"

We all chuckled as we headed out the door of our room and walked down the palm-lined path to the ferry that would take us to the park. It was another balmy, breezy day in the Bahamas. The sunrays glittering on the turquoise water looked postcard-worthy.

It was nice to be in paradise. I missed my sweet puppers, Marlon, but the vibe here was a balm to my soul. As I settled on the padded bench seat of the ferry, I fluffed out my pink dress. My hand flew to my neck, where my castle pendant sparkled in the sunshine.

6

PRYCE

"Wow, it's late. I didn't mean to sleep so long," Evan groaned when he looked at the clock on the nightstand next to his bed. He threw a pillow my way, which bounced right off my head.

I was in my own bed watching the stock market ticker scroll by. I'd just finished reading an article on the resurgence of the Greek Revival architectural style. *A revival revival, if you will.* "What was that for?"

"Why'd you let me sleep so late?" He scooted up in the bed, rubbing his eyes. The last few words were garbled due to a giant yawn spreading his mouth so wide I could practically see his tonsils.

"Sorry, I didn't realize I'm supposed to be your human alarm clock. I thought I was supposed to be on vacation." I rolled my eyes. "What's on the agenda today?"

"Well, it's our divorce trip," he reminded me—like I'd

somehow forgotten. "Yesterday we rode the rides. Today, we could either drink ourselves silly, or we could try to get laid. I mean, we could try to do both, but the latter might be challenging with whiskey dick."

"Speak for yourself." I chuckled. "I don't suffer from that affliction."

"You must not be drinking as much as I do, then." He threw back the sheet, and I was stunned to see he was sporting enormous morning wood.

"Hey, ever hear of clothes?" I complained as I made a big show of averting my eyes. It was mostly a joke, though, because I'd always considered myself to be a bit bi-curious. Maybe this trip would be a good time to explore that side of me. Not with Evan though, even though I knew he swung that way too. We were almost like brothers, though.

"You love it, don't lie." He stood next to my bed and swung his dick around and then grabbed his balls. "I'm gonna go shower."

"Good idea." I pulled up the Spicetopia website on my phone. Getting laid was definitely at the top of my to-do list for today. I scanned the site to see where the best venue for making that happen might be. That was where I discovered Kink Link.

By the time Evan got out of the shower, I had my own morning wood just from fantasizing about all the vast possibilities we could explore at the park today. I tried to cover it with the sheet and blanket when he walked back into the room with a towel wrapped around his waist.

"So, what do you think?" A bead of water dripped down his muscular torso.

"Two words," I carefully enunciated, "Kink Link."

"Oh, yeah, I was looking at that yesterday. That's the place where you enter all your information into a computer, and it matches you with people who want to explore the same kink as you, right?"

"That's the one." I winked. Thankfully his presence was making my stiffy go down. I swung my legs over the bed. "I'll shower, then we can head out."

He removed the towel and started to dry off. "Let's get a big breakfast first. I'm starving."

"We definitely need to fuel up," I agreed. "Hopefully we'll be burning lots of calories today."

He flexed his biceps and grinned. "I like that plan!"

I STOOD in front of the computer for a while, debating what my responses should be. Part of me thought a simple vanilla encounter—just me and a beautiful lady—fit the bill. Another part of me wanted to explore things I never could have done with my ex. Dana wasn't exactly adventurous.

I'm at Spicetopia—where Variety is the Spice of Life! I repeated the park's tagline in my head like a mantra, giving myself the courage to push the envelope. I put in my top two interests as domination and exhibitionism, then waited for it to spit out my results.

For a moment, I just stared at the slip of paper that printed out. Evan had already gotten his results and gone off to find his match. I must have stood there for a while because a Spicetopia staff member approached with a smile plastered on her face.

"Good morning! Can I help you figure out the next step?" Her tone was pleasant, but my mind still translated it as, *Come on, dumbass, you're holding up the line. Let's get you where you need to go.*

I smiled back at her and waved my printed slip. "Oh, sure. It says Room 82?"

"That's the room you should go to," she explained. "Once you get there, there's a short debriefing. Then the divider will part, and you'll meet the person or people you're matched with. You'll have a few moments to talk about boundaries, establish a safe word, and basically make sure you're on the same page. You're in one of the exhibition rooms, so if you choose to make that part of your scene, one wall will turn transparent after you press the button, so those in the voyeur hall will be able to watch. Do you have any questions?"

That seemed pretty clear and straightforward. "Thanks," I glanced at her name badge, "Marcy, and where is Room 82?"

She used her whole hand to point down a corridor on my left. "Straight down that hall, Rooms 80-100."

After thanking her again, I made my way to the designated room. Wow, they had at least a hundred rooms for people to get their freak on. Spicetopia was simply incredible!

A mixture of emotions was flooding my body: excitement, apprehension, sudden shyness—the latter, I hadn't anticipated at all. I'd done some BDSM-type stuff with a girl I dated right out of college. I liked the dominant side of me—but my ex-wife did not. I wondered if it would come right out, or if it would need to be coaxed.

When I got to the room, I scanned the barcode on my printout under the reader, and the door slid open like something on a spaceship. The room was small but comfortable, with a sofa, a spanking bench, and a cabinet of sorts that I assumed contained props, condoms, lube, et cetera. A screen opened in the wall, and a video explained exactly what Marcy had just told me but in more depth.

I wondered what Evan was doing. He'd told me he was going to search for a partner interested in anal sex—that was what he was in the mood for, and his ex was adamantly opposed to any and all butt stuff. We apparently both wanted to explore things we weren't able to do in our previous relationships. I supposed that was the beauty of a divorce trip to Spicetopia.

Before I could ponder any further, the divider in front of me moved up into the ceiling, and a space opened up that mirrored mine and doubled the size of the room. On the small sofa across from me sat a woman.

My heart rate rocketed into the stratosphere as I looked her up and down. She smiled and leaned forward, pressing her ample breasts together with her arms. She licked her lips and raked her dark, cat-shaped eyes from my head to my toes. Then she stood up and approached me.

It hit me all of the sudden that this was wrong.

Dead wrong.

I didn't want to do this. I didn't want to do *her*.

"Where's the abort mission button?" I questioned, panic in my voice as I sprang to my feet. My eyes darted around the room as the woman's lips curled down and her brows drew together.

"What's wrong?" She stroked her fingers down her body—which was gorgeous, really. She was conventionally beautiful. Long jet-black hair. Exquisite pale skin covering full lips, hips and breasts. Her dark eyes looked like they held a million secrets.

"I'm sorry, I just—it's not you," I stammered, "it's me. I'm so sorry..."

7

PENNY

I sat alone in the little room they directed me to after filling out the Kink Link questionnaire. Ben and Yvonne had moved to the voyeur's hall. Before I left, Ben reached for my hand and guided it to his pants. "I'm so hard thinking about you getting manhandled by someone," he said. "I can't wait to watch."

I laughed. "I'll do my best to entertain you." Having been a hard-core theater geek when I was in high school, I did find the prospect of turning people on just by performing for them rather titillating. Not to mention, the anticipation of discovering a new partner was doing crazy things to my own southern hemisphere.

Yvonne leaned in and pressed a kiss to my cheek. "I know you'll do great, Penny, but you're sure you want to do this, right?"

My eyes darted between theirs, looking so eager and hopeful I'd agree. "Yeah, of course I do."

I hadn't been with another man since I'd met them, which had been six months ago now. I'd be lying if I said I didn't sometimes fantasize about being with someone other than Ben or Yvonne. And it wasn't like I'd been exclusive with them—not yet, anyway. I could go out and date whoever I wanted. But I liked our dynamic and thought it was a good fit for me, especially for the stage of life I was in now, settled in my career and looking for routine and stability.

I wanted to please them.

I enjoyed pleasing my partners.

Even more than I enjoyed receiving pleasure.

I watched the instructional video, and, at the end, the host reassured that it was always okay to stop the action. "Consent may be withdrawn at any time," she explained. "Simply speak your safe word, and all action must stop immediately. Or, if speaking your safe word is not possible, there are emergency buttons on each wall, about a foot off the floor. They are located above the electrical outlets."

Hmm, good to know, I thought to myself, but I didn't anticipate needing to use them.

The hostess finished her spiel, and the panel between my room and the adjoining one slid up. A man stood there—about my height, with lean limbs covered in tattoos that contrasted with his pale skin. He wore a black leather vest and skin-tight jeans with a chain hanging from one of his belt loops.

He eyed me up and down. "Hey, gorgeous."

I didn't know what came over me, but I panicked. My heart raced, goosebumps and a cold sweat erupting on my skin.

He wasn't unattractive. He just—

Wasn't for me.

My hands flew up to cover my gasp as I realized, in that moment, I didn't want to fuck a random guy. I just had zero interest in it. Clutching the pendant around my neck, I shook my head, apologizing profusely to the man standing before me.

"Hey, where are you going?" he called after me as I continued backing toward the door.

I hit the red button, and it slid open. I was still shaking and muttering, "I'm so sorry. Please forgive me," when I stumbled out of the door and literally ran right into a huge, hulking body.

The impact sent me sprawling to the floor, my heart pounding and confusion swirling in my head.

When I looked up, a hazy figure was towering over me.

"PENNY?" He stepped back and lowered his hand to help me to my feet.

Standing before me was the man who'd watched me eat a snow cone the night before. "Pryce?"

His eyes immediately snapped to the castle pendant Pryce had given me years ago. "You still have it. It *is* you…" He shook his head like he couldn't quite believe it himself.

"Wh-what are you doing here?" I stammered, staring up at him in awe. He had to be six-three or six-four—he obviously had a huge growth spurt after we met. His formerly shaggy gold surfer hair was cropped shorter and was a darker blond, but those angular chocolate-brown eyes and sharp cheekbones were the exact same. He wore baggy khaki shorts and a faded blue Foo Fighters concert tee.

My heart felt like it might explode right out of my chest at any given moment, it was pounding so hard under my ribs. I could barely hear over the sound of blood rushing through my ears. Disoriented from the fall and the weird design of this building, I considered pinching myself to make sure I wasn't dreaming.

He grinned at me, those familiar dark eyes shining. "I came with a friend—we're celebrating our divorces."

I looked at him, blinking several times. "You came to Spicetopia with someone you just divorced?"

"Oh, no, we weren't married to each other. We both just got divorced—we were married to different people. I mean, we were already friends and just happened to be going through a divorce at the same time, so we, uh…" he rambled on. Then his lips stretched into a wide smile, and he shook his head as though he was struggling to process what was happening.

My lungs burned as I huffed out a sharp sigh, fully understanding his apparent discombobulation. After all, it felt like there'd been a rip in the space-time continuum. I finally managed to comment, "I see. I guess that makes sense."

"What about you? I thought I saw you last night, but I

—" He couldn't tear his eyes away from me. They pierced right through me like laser beams. "You disappeared before I could really talk to you. I thought I—

At the same time, I blurted, "I thought I—"

"—imagined you," we both said together.

"Can we talk more? Is that possible?" His head turned from side to side as he surveyed the space we were in, a narrow hallway between rooms with gray walls and doors as far as the eye could see. "Can we go someplace else...to talk?"

I glanced around too and was about to suggest figuring out a way to get outside when I remembered Ben and Yvonne. And, unsurprisingly, it was just about that time my phone buzzed—Yvonne was calling me.

What would she and Ben think about me wanting to spend time alone with Pryce?

And I did want to spend time *alone* with him. Every fiber of my being was begging me to get reacquainted with him.

But possibly even more important: what would Pryce think about the fact I was here with a couple?

8

PRYCE

I couldn't believe Penny was standing right in front of me. Even though it had been eons since I'd seen her—and I only knew her for a short amount of time—I'd never forgotten her. She drifted in and out of my fantasies like the moon on a cloudy night.

I was about to see if I could find an empty room here in Kink Link to drag her into when her phone rang. She looked flustered, scrambling for her phone, her chest heaving with rapid breaths.

"Hello?" she answered, those beautiful mounds rising and falling with each intake of air. I wanted to run my tongue between her cleavage so bad...

Okay, I felt bad for eavesdropping, but I also wanted to know who was calling her at Spicetopia and, more importantly, why she was answering. Was she here alone? She didn't say. I sure fumbled explaining my own situation, though, didn't I? I should have made up something, like I was here for an architectural convention. Yeah, that would have been better.

"I'm fine. Yeah, I just chickened out. Hey, listen, would you mind if I met up with you later?" Another pause. "Yeah, everything is good. I'd like to—" She giggled, and a pink blush spread across her freckled cheeks. That fact she still had freckles melted my heart. "Of course I will. I can take care of myself, you know." Eyeroll. "Okay, fine. Yeah."

She slipped the phone back into the hot pink purse strapped across her body. "Sorry about that."

I forced my gaze away from her mouthwatering cleavage and back to her turquoise eyes. "No need to apologize. Everything good?"

Her eyes sparkled like the depths of the sea basking beneath a golden sun. "Yep. Wanna go catch up?"

"Yeah, we'll grab a drink and see where things go." I did the gentlemanly thing of offering her the crook of my arm.

This time, those beautiful, seductive eyes raked up and down my body, her thick, dark lashes fluttering. "Actually, I have a better idea."

I sure hoped it involved my lips on hers and my hands exploring that breathtaking body. If I thought she had decadent curves when she was fourteen, now she was a full-fledged goddess of curves.

She grabbed my hand and pulled me down the hall. My dick leapt to attention, pressing painfully into the zipper on my shorts.

When my phone buzzed in my pocket, I had a feeling

it was Evan, but I wasn't about to distract Penny from finding us a place to fuck, if that was indeed her goal. She was definitely a lot more forward than I remembered her being, and I was here for it. I remembered Evan admonishing me to lighten up and have some fun—he insisted I shouldn't be so *serious* all the time. This seemed like the perfect opportunity for me to shed my stuffy persona and let loose. *Won't Evan be proud?*

Penny marched right up to a Spicetopia employee and flashed a smile. "Hi, is there a place here in the park where two people can go just to have some privacy?"

"Sure." The young woman grinned back and held out her iPad showing a park map. "The cabanas at the beach are private. There are also booths at the Glory Hole, the Peep Show Theatre, and the Adult Emporium. I can call over and reserve a space for you, if you'd like."

Penny batted her long, thick fringe of eyelashes and studied the map. "So, what's closest to here? The Glory Hole?"

"Yes. Just a moment." The employee, whose name badge read Daisy, pressed a button on her iPad and then spoke into the headset she was wearing. "Private room for two. About ten minutes? Sure, of course. Yes. Thank you." She pressed another button and then lifted her gaze to us. "You're all set. Just tell them Daisy called ahead for you."

"Thank you so much!" Penny practically squealed, and then she took off down the hall like a streak of pink lightning—only to get to the end of the corridor and have no idea how to get out of the building. Another staff member saw our rush and opened an emergency exit for us, shooting us a knowing look.

We walked down the lush path flanked by sweet-smelling tropical plants and bushes until we got to Main Street. From there, we just had to go a couple of buildings down toward the park entrance before The Glory Hole came into view. The façade looked like a very proper Georgian-style brick building with tall windows that sported colorful stained-glass transoms.

"I would've never thought I'd set foot in The Glory Hole." I laughed, and she glanced over her shoulder at me, looking unsure for the first time since we'd been reacquainted.

She stopped on a dime and whipped around to face me. "Are you having second thoughts?"

"Oh hell no." I held the door open and ushered her inside. The interior was all dark mahogany, ornate lighting fixtures, and crimson velvet drapes, and there was a deep, exotic musky scent emanating from two enormous tropical floral arrangements on either side of the reception area.

We went straight up to the sleek pink and white marble-topped desk. "We reserved a private room for two? Daisy sent us."

"Of course. Right this way." The staff member—Tyrell, according to his name badge—opened a velvet rope and gestured for us to follow him. We journeyed down a long hallway with doors on both sides. It almost looked like a hotel. Then we stopped in front of Room 17. When he swiped a key card on a pad, the door clicked open.

"Enjoy," he said, not a trace of judgment in his voice. He was likely used to hooking couples up with a space to, well, hook up.

I let Penny enter first, and she immediately whipped around to face me, a sultry smile spreading her lips. "I can't believe I'm standing here with you at Spicetopia."

I took two steps toward her and stroked a finger down her cheek. "Me either. I still don't understand how we lost touch all those years ago."

She shook her head, her fire-red hair swishing over her shoulders. "It's not important now. It was a different time—no cell phones, no social media. It was much harder to stay in touch with people who lived far away. Maryland to Texas might as well have been from here to the moon."

I chuckled as I wrapped my arms around her. "True... There are so many things I've dreamed of doing to you. I've been dreaming about you for twenty years, you know."

She spread her arms wide. "No need to dream any longer—I'm here now. You can do anything you want to me."

"Anything?" I flashed her a wicked grin.

"Anything." Her lips curled into a smirk, and then she ran the tip of her tongue around them before her bottom lip tucked under her teeth.

Just looking at her mouth made my cock strain against the front of my shorts, begging to burst out. I wanted to take my time with her, but I didn't know if I could hold out. Desire coursed through me with such urgency, I felt like that same teen boy who nearly came in his swim trunks the first time we made out.

This whole time—for over twenty years now—I'd fantasized about what it would be like to slide into her pussy, how she would feel clenching around me, milking my cock. And I was finally going to find out.

"Let's start with a kiss," I suggested. "I want to see if your lips are as magical as they were when we were kids."

"Mmm...sounds like a good place to begin." Her eyes fluttered closed as I tilted my face toward her, brushing my lips softly against hers. Then I ran the tip of my tongue along the seam between her lips, just like I did all those years ago in the Sweetopia resort pool. When she parted them, I tentatively delved inside as a moan rumbled up from deep in her throat.

My fingers tangled in her long, copper-colored tresses as she melted in my arms, giving herself over to the intensity of our kiss. Each breath she exhaled, I swallowed down, hungry for more—more of her lips, more of her luscious curves.

She was wearing a ruffled pink sundress that showcased her heavenly breasts, and in my haste, I practically ripped it off her. At the last second, I stopped myself from tearing the fabric, remembering we had to walk out of here with the necessary bits covered—the only place full-on nudity was allowed at Spicetopia was on the nude beach. After I dispatched the dress, she stood before me in a strapless flesh-colored satin bra and a matching thong that hugged her full hips and separated the two voluptuous hemispheres of her ass.

I reached behind her and deftly unfastened the bra, letting it drop to the floor at our feet. "I didn't think it was possible for you to be more beautiful than you were when we were younger," I whispered in her ear as my hands cupped her breasts, kneading the soft flesh. She threw her head back, gasping at the sensation. "But here we are, and you are."

"When I got home from Sweetopia all those years ago, I regretted not giving you my virginity," she admitted, her eyes hooded with lust as they roamed my face. Then her gaze dropped to watch my fingers pinch and pull at her hard pink nipples. "I wish we would have gone all the way, but I was scared—"

"And I didn't push the issue," I added. "I wanted you to ask me. But it doesn't matter now. I don't care if you've been with a hundred men, this is *our* first time together."

The years that had elapsed between our first meeting at Sweetopia and our reunion at Spicetopia were irrelevant. All that mattered was this present moment, and I was finally going to find out what it felt like to be inside her.

I pushed her down onto the soft velvet chaise, then dropped to the floor and simultaneously spread her knees wide. She looked down at me with a plea in her eyes.

"Are you ready for me to taste you?" I asked the question she had already answered with the intense desire burning in her pupils.

She managed to rasp out, "Please, Pryce, fuck… I'm so wet…it's dripping down my thighs."

I bent my head, inspecting her. A crown of silky red curls sat atop her soft, rounded mound, and below it were the sweetest pink lips I'd ever seen. I parted them with a finger, exposing her swollen nub, and I couldn't stop my tongue from flicking it, sparking a shudder through her whole body. Her thighs clenched, and a moan hummed out of her mouth.

Taking my time, I licked up her seam, circled her clit, and then trailed my tongue back down as she squirmed and sighed. Reaching underneath her, I gripped her ass, one cheek in each hand, lifting her pussy to my mouth so I could eat it like a starved man.

I had never tasted anything so delicious in my life. I could easily become addicted to her taste—*talk about Sweetopia...*

"You're gonna make me come," she gritted out between clenched teeth, and as soon as she got the words out, her eyes rolled back in her head. Her pussy gushed all over my face as she convulsed in my arms. It was the single hottest thing I had ever witnessed in my life.

I worried I might lose my battle not to come in my pants—it was like being fifteen all over again. My cock throbbed and ached for her, my balls tight and heavy with cum I wanted to shoot deep inside her.

I hoped I would be able to get her off at least one more time before finding my own relief. This was an orgasm twenty years in the making, and I didn't know if I could wait a second longer.

9

PENNY

*W*atching Pryce wipe my juices off his chin, looking as satisfied as if he'd been the one who climaxed, I smiled. That boy who straddled the line between cocky and shy had grown into a man who was self-assured and masterfully skilled in the fine art of cunnilingus. If he was that talented with his tongue, I could only imagine his cock was every bit as talented.

"Fuck, Pryce, that was—" I shook my head, my chest still heaving with short, gasping breaths. "I can't even complete a fucking thought." Bracing my hands on the chaise, I struggled to sit up. Cool air fanned against my inner thighs, highlighting the wetness that had gathered there.

He stood up and gripped his cock through his shorts. "I need you, Penny, fuck… You have me so hard."

"I wanna see." I licked my lips as he showed off the

outline of his erection straining against the thin khaki fabric. When we were younger and made out, I'd felt him pressing against me, but I never actually saw it or touched it. It felt massive then, and I remembered being scared to death of it.

I wasn't scared now, though.

Until he unfastened his pants, and the biggest cock I'd ever seen in my life unfurled from his boxers. Okay, I still wasn't nervous because it looked thick and mouthwatering, and I knew I'd feel so amazing being completely filled up by that massive tool.

I leaned forward and fisted the thing—couldn't get my fingers to meet my thumb. It pulsed in my hand as I squeezed, and Pryce's head tipped back, a growl emanating from his throat. When I stroked up his shaft, a pearly bead of pre-cum oozed out the slit. My tongue darted out to taste his salty essence.

Fuck, this was going to be fun. I couldn't wait to watch him fall apart. He'd given me an orgasm with his fingers when I was fourteen, and it was high time I returned the favor.

Just when I started to wrap my lips around the thing, he shoved me back against the chaise. "I'm sorry, that feels amazing, but I'm gonna blow my load, and I wanna do it inside you."

"Holy fuck, that's the hottest sentence I've ever heard." My voice was barely more than a breathy whisper.

Just when I was about to spread my legs so he could guide himself inside, a speaker in our room crackled to life. I jumped so high, I nearly hit the ceiling, and Pryce sprang back as if he'd received an electric shock.

"Pardon the interruption," a smooth, deep voice said, and I couldn't tell if it was human or robot at first, to be honest. "Your party is waiting for you at the front desk. They are concerned—can you please check in?" It had to be Tyrell at the front desk.

"Party?" Pryce blinked, his nostrils flaring and chest heaving. He fisted his cock as though he couldn't stand not to have pressure against it.

"What party?" I asked, not sure if Tyrell could hear me.

"They say their names are Ben and Yvonne?"

Fuck.

"Who's that? What's wrong?" Pryce scrambled to his feet, his stiff cock jutting up against his abs. Was that thing gonna go down on its own, or did we have one of those four-hour Viagra situations going on here?

"Tell them I'll be out in a few minutes," I told Tyrell.

"Thank you. Again, sorry for the interruption," his deep voiced returned. "They were concerned about your safety, and we take safety very seriously here at Spicetopia."

The look of confusion on Pryce's face caused a stab of guilt to ricochet through me. "It's..." I sighed. "It's complicated."

He started to pull on his boxer briefs and shorts. "What do you mean, complicated? I thought you were free to...you know..."

"I am," I insisted. "I'm in an open relationship with a couple. I can do whatever I want; it's just—"

"You're in a relationship?" The hurt in his eyes was unmistakable. "But I thought—"

"It's not an exclusive relationship," I explained carefully. "I mean, it's not yet... This trip was supposed to be—"

"You lied to me." He threw his blue Foo Fighters shirt over his head and worked his thick, muscular arms through the holes. "Why did you come to The Glory Hole with me if you're in a relationship with a couple?"

I shook my head, wishing I could slow down time so I could get my bearings and explain this in a way he could understand, accept. "Pryce, wait. Please? We just reconnected; I don't want to—"

"I wish I'd never run into you." His eyes narrowed and lips thinned as he slipped on his sandals.

And with that, he stormed out the door, not even bothering to look back or say goodbye.

My heart sank. Why didn't he give me a chance to explain?

Standing in the empty room, I considered my options. But there was nothing I could do now except put my bra, dress, and panties back on and go out to meet Ben and Yvonne.

THE WALK to the front desk felt like the walk of shame. When I saw Ben and Yvonne's relieved faces, guilt churned in my stomach again. Not that I had done anything to them I should feel guilty about, but—

I realized in that moment I couldn't give them what they wanted, what they hoped would be the natural outcome of our time at Spicetopia: an exclusive relationship. A committed throuple relationship.

Not to mention the fact that I apparently couldn't make *anyone* happy today.

And that stung. Because I loved pleasing people, making people happy. But I couldn't do it if it was going to be at my own expense.

"Are you okay? Was the guy who just flounced outta here the dude you were with?" Yvonne blurted out as Ben pulled me into his arms, squeezing me so tight, my lungs nearly popped.

"That was Pryce," I confirmed, wiggling out of Ben's embrace. "Can we go somewhere to talk?"

"Pryce?" Yvonne's eyebrows shot up. "Not Pryce who gave you the necklace? It really was him?"

Confusion washed across Ben's face as he stood there staring at me, lips parted, his chest rising and falling with heavy breaths. Did they run here?

Pretending to study his iPad, Tyrell was obviously intrigued but was doing his level best to look like he wasn't eavesdropping on our drama. I could only imagine the things he saw here on a daily basis.

"Sure, of course. Who is Pryce, by the way?" Ben asked. "The guy you hooked up with at Kink Link?"

"I'll explain later." I shook my head as Yvonne reached down and took my hand into hers.

Ben headed toward the door, looking over his shoulder as he spoke, "We made reservations for lunch at the Stimulate Your Senses Restaurant across the way. We just got nervous when you didn't answer your texts or a call, and—"

He reached the front door of The Glory Hole just as it swung open and a figure entered. The two men collided with a thud, pushing Ben backwards into Yvonne and me. Petite Yvonne bounced off me and went flying into one of the velvet sofas in the lobby.

"Oh no, I'm so sorry!" The man with a shiny bald head and tall, wiry build seemed panicked. He rushed over to Yvonne and offered a hand to help her up. "Are you okay? I didn't mean to—"

"I'm fine," Yvonne insisted, smoothing her tiny shorts down as she stood up. "Are you okay? You look flustered."

"Sorry, I think my buddy was in here a few minutes ago. Lost track of him at Kink Link about an hour ago. We had Life 360 turned on, but he just turned it off. This is the last place I had a location for him. Maybe you saw him here? He's tall, blondish-brown hair, tan skin, scruff on his—"

"Pryce?" I blurted out.

The bald man cocked his head, brows pulled together. "Yeah, that's him. How'd you know his name?"

"I'm Penny," I introduced myself. "We knew each other when we were kids. I upset him—that's why he left." I blew out a breath and shuffled my wedge-heeled sandal against the plush Persian rug in The Glory Hole's lobby. I realized this friend might be my key to getting Pryce's number so I could apologize. Maybe I did mislead him, but I didn't mean to. We had probably exchanged more bodily fluids than words since we ran into each other an hour ago.

I looked up at the bald man with the charming smile I usually reserved for sweet-talking my principal into letting me do something I wanted to do in my classroom. "Hey, maybe you'd like to come to lunch with us? I could explain what happened to all of you." I sighed. "I'm sorry to cause such a mess, guys."

"I'm Evan," he said, stretching his hand out for me to shake. "That's kind of you to offer, and I just happen to be starving. Pryce and I were supposed to head to lunch after the Kink Link, but I seemed to have lost touch with him. He's not answering his phone either."

"I ruined everything," I confessed, feeling embarrassed that Pryce and I had sabotaged so many people's afternoons by acting like horny teens.

"Yes, let's go have lunch," Ben suggested, "and we can iron all of this out." He wrapped his arm around my shoulder, and, on the other side of me, Yvonne continued to hold my hand, squeezing it tightly in hers.

Evan followed the three of us out of The Glory Hole and down the sidewalk to the nearby restaurant, seeming more relaxed now and not nearly as concerned about his buddy being MIA.

I was grateful for Ben's level head and Yvonne's generous spirit, I just hoped they would forgive me when they learned what I'd decided. And I hoped Pryce would forgive me for putting my libido before my words.

Fate had brought us back together again, but why? I didn't want to fuck it up before I could find out the answer to that question.

10

PRYCE

*a*s I was leaving The Glory Hole, my phone rang. *Evan.*

No, I didn't want to talk to him right now, and I didn't want to see him either. I turned off my phone so he couldn't track me down. I just needed to be alone right now. To stew. Or brood. Or something. Fuck!

I honestly didn't know who I was more angry with— Penny or myself.

And why was I angry in the first place? Why did I storm out of The Glory Hole? We were about to do it. I was mere moments away from fulfilling a fantasy twenty years in the making, and I got completely bent out of shape because Penny's boyfriend and girlfriend came looking for her?

Why the hell should I care? I should have just fucked her!

What was my primary purpose in visiting Spicetopia? To fuck! And Penny had been on my Most Wanted Fuck List since I was fifteen years old. So what was the actual fucking problem?

Did I ask Penny if she was seeing anyone?

I couldn't remember exactly, but shouldn't she have volunteered that information? She said she was dating a couple? Did that mean she was bisexual?

Wait! What the hell difference does it make?

It wasn't like I was going home with her. It wasn't like we were going to start a relationship. It would have just been a fun little fling—just like it was twenty fucking years ago.

So, why did it bother me so much that she was there with a couple?

I walked down Main Street toward the entrance gates. I was thinking of just heading to the dock and taking the ferry back to the hotel, which was on a separate island from the theme park. But then the Peep Show Theatre caught my eye, and I decided to check it out. Some mindless entertainment might be just what the doctor ordered.

The building reminded me of the famous Chinese Theatre in Hollywood with its plush red velvet lobby, elegant mosaic tile and ornate gold trim on everything. The murals in the back depicted various sexual acts, illustrated in a stunning Asian-inspired style. There looked to be five separate theaters. I paused at the small unstaffed desk to see where I should go.

One theater was a huge auditorium, but since it was daytime, nothing was happening on stage. According to the sign, the venue offered burlesque shows, Chippendales-style male revues, erotic demonstrations like shibari and other BDSM techniques, and entertainment every evening. The other four theaters were smaller, more like screening rooms. The first was for viewing classic porn clips; the second was for contemporary porn. The third one featured LGBTQ porn, and the fourth theater showed fetish porn.

I slipped into the classic porn theater, not knowing what to expect. The clip playing when I sank into the soft velvet seat was apparently from the 80s, as evidenced by the music, the spandex, and the Magnum PI-style 'stache on the dude. It wasn't really arousing—more amusing, to be honest.

I even chuckled at the cheesy dialogue. It was a good distraction from what had just happened with Penny, but I needed to decide what to do about her.

And what to do about me.

After all, I was the real problem here, right? I got upset and overreacted, and I couldn't figure out why it bothered me so much.

I thought I was here to get some closure after my divorce. Spicetopia was the place to sow some wild oats, enjoy a couple good fucks, and then I was going back to Houston to find the woman of my dreams, so we could settle down and start a family.

Was the reason I was so upset that Penny was at Spice-topia with other partners and didn't tell me because I wanted something more with her than just a fuck?

I was here for a good time, not to find the love of my life. But in the back of my mind, I'd always wondered if Penny and I couldn't have had something. We never got the chance to try, living so far apart in an era when it wasn't easy to stay in touch.

No one was more surprised than me that she was suddenly back in my life, the girl I had carried a torch for since high school. The one who'd gotten away.

Was a relationship something she would even consider? Or was I crazy for even thinking about it?

Well, she obviously *wasn't* interested if she was already in a relationship with a couple. And *I* wasn't interested if she couldn't be honest with me. And she *wasn't* honest, was she? I told her why I was here... She had every opportunity to do the same.

Twenty years had passed, and I still thought about her regularly. When I saw her today, my heart felt like it might explode out of my chest. Not only was she absolutely stunning, but I felt an immediate connection to her, like what we'd developed all those years ago was still there, perfectly preserved. Like we could just pick up where we'd left off, as though two decades hadn't passed.

I remembered thinking, *I'm single again, and she's single too. This is clearly meant to be. Fate.*

Why would Fate put Penny back in my life if it wasn't some sort of sign?

That thought rumbled through my mind the entire time we were walking from Kink Link to The Glory Hole. From everything she was saying and doing, it seemed like she was on the exact same page. And when we shared our second first kiss, my post-divorce and Spicetopia goals sort of flew out the window.

So that was what happened. Clearly. My agenda for Spicetopia was replaced with something intrinsic, some deep-seated compulsion to see if second chances were fate leading you down the path you were always meant to take.

That was why I was so shocked to hear she was visiting Spicetopia with a couple. A couple!

It is kind of hot now that I think about it.

I blew out an exasperated breath. I didn't give her much of a chance to explain.

In my defense, during our last conversation, most of the blood that was supposed to be flowing to my brain and making it work had been trapped in my massive erection—which had finally subsided thanks to the gut-punch I received when I heard about her relationship. And this cheesy 80s porn was definitely not resurrecting it!

Now that I could think clearly, it was all starting to crystalize. I didn't give her a chance to explain, and I didn't even get her number. Maybe her Spicetopia goals also went to shit as soon as she saw we had a second chance? But how would I ever know?

I was a fucking dumbass. How was I going to just serendipitously run into her again? I didn't want to wait another twenty years for it to happen—that was for sure.

Was there a way to get a message to her? Could someone at Guest Services contact her on my behalf?

I stood up, leaving the 80s porn behind to head over to Guest Services, which was next door. I'd see if they could track down a Penelope—

Wait.

Did I remember her last name?

Did she even have the same last name she had at fourteen?

Fuck!

There was a massive fountain between the theater and Main Street of a voluptuous goddess with her legs spread and water erupting from between her thighs like she was squirting gallons of lady cum a second. All around her were smaller jets shooting into the air, and when I looked closer, I saw they were actually phallic. *Very eye-catching.*

I sat down on one of the benches and took out my phone. After turning it on, I saw I'd missed three calls and four texts from Evan. I texted him back:

> Me: Hey, I'm outside Guest Services. Sorry for going MIA.

> Evan: It's okay. We still on for dinner tonight?

> Me: I'm not in a great mood, but I guess so.

> Evan: This place is world-renowned. Trust me, you don't want to miss it.

> Me: Fine. I'll see you there.

11

PENNY

*W*e all shuffled into the Stimulate Your Senses restaurant, and I was immediately taken in by the theming. It was designed to engage the senses, and it certainly lived up to the hype. Complex patterns and a riot of colors presented a feast for the eyes, while the textures of the walls, seating, fixtures and floors were unexpected and made you want to reach out and touch them. Pleasantly appetizing and mildly erotic scents wafted in the air, while soothing music filtered into my ears with a beat that made me want to move.

"Can we change our reservation from three people to four?" Ben asked the hostess, who was wearing a vibrant yellow vinyl jumpsuit. Her long black hair was pulled into a ponytail so sleek, it looked like a satin waterfall. Speaking of waterfalls, water features were built into the walls on either side of the space.

"You'll be seated in the Sound Room; is that to your liking?" she asked, consulting her iPad.

"Sure, of course," Ben agreed with a nod, then looked at all of us to confirm. I had no idea what that entailed, so I just went along with it. So did Yvonne and our newcomer, Evan.

Next thing I knew, Ben was slipping a satin blindfold over my eyes and guiding me to a low cushion on the floor. As the darkness settled and my other senses adjusted, I found myself immersed in sounds that shifted like colors in a kaleidoscope. First it was jungle noises, with screeching birds and the purr of a tiger. Then came ocean sounds: soothing waves crashing on a distant beach while seagulls squawked in the distance. Next it was raindrops plinking on a metal roof.

"You can take the blindfolds off to look at the menu," the server explained, "or to talk, or whatever, but we find they enhance the experience." She left us alone to debate our meal choices, and we all sat there for several long moments, soaking up the exquisite, exotic rhythms and melodies of the diverse recordings.

I finished listening to a segment that put me in the midst of a full symphony orchestra as they performed. Then I tentatively raised my blindfold to find that the other three members of our party were all staring at me.

"Thanks for joining us, Penny," Yvonne teased me, stroking her hand down my thigh. "Care to fill us in about what's going on?"

Last night, I'd sort of explained to Yvonne how I'd met Pryce at Sweetopia when we were kids, but I rehashed the story for Ben and Evan. Evan was smiling the whole time, apparently amused thinking of his buddy as a teen. Yvonne's hand now rested on Evan's knee, and every once in a while, they shared a look.

Hmmm. Looks like some senses might be getting stimulated right at this table...

"So, why did you just leave him hanging there in The Glory Hole room?" Ben asked. "Dude has to have a serious case of blue balls."

Evan and Yvonne both laughed while I rolled my eyes. "Because y'all interrupted us, that's why. It really caught us both off guard and sort of ruined the moment."

"Sheesh, sorry!" Ben was now the one rolling his eyes.

I continued, "Then, when I explained to Pryce that I was here with a couple... Well, I guess I'd neglected to tell him earlier because we'd been so caught up in each other. He was downright pissed. He is the one who stormed out, so if he has blue balls, that's on him."

"So, is he mad because you're polyamorous or...?" Yvonne interjected.

I shrugged. "I was trying to explain the situation when he stormed out. In my defense, all my blood had diverted much farther south of my brain, and I wasn't having the easiest time putting words together. And then, of course, I also failed to get his number, so I can't even get in touch to apologize."

I pushed out a long, heavy sigh just as the server returned with our drinks. This was good because I was craving a nice buzz. Could I just enjoy a liquid lunch and perhaps forget I ever ran into my long-lost first crush?

Everything was so simple when we were kids at Sweetopia.

"Sounds like you and Pryce need to talk things out," Evan declared.

I shot him a look that very clearly said "duh," and he immediately put his blindfold back on. "Oh, she's just teasing you," Yvonne soothed him, stroking her hands down his back.

Evan recovered quickly, sliding the blindfold back down and giving me a megawatt grin. "I'm sure I can put you in touch with him. I mean—if that's what you want." He stretched out his arm until it was wrapped around Yvonne, who didn't hesitate to snuggle into his embrace.

Ben's gaze shot toward his wife, his eyes narrowing. He clearly didn't approve of Yvonne flirting with Evan. Then he turned a serious expression toward me. "So what *do* you want, Penny? Where does this leave us?"

I stared at him for a moment, my mouth opening and closing like a fish out of water gasping for a breath.

"Look, you need to be honest with us." Yvonne leaned toward the table and pinned her eyes on me. "We've always been honest with you about what we want, but if what *we* want isn't what *you* want—"

"I don't think I'm ready to be committed to a couple," I blurted out.

I instantly realized I *didn't* say "be committed to *anyone*."

Because, in the back of my mind, I was still working out whether or not there was any chance Pryce and I had a strong enough connection to…you know, make a go at a relationship.

It was silly, right? To be thinking of him that way

when we only knew each other as kids, not as adults. But why were my mind and heart racing with the idea of it?

A deep breath fanned out as the burden weighing me down seemed to lift. Both Ben's and Yvonne's faces fell. Evan still had a goofy grin on his face like a dog with a brand-new bone.

I needed to give my lovers more—a reason. "I wanted to be ready to commit. I liked the idea of building something with the two of you. I liked the security and the routine of it. And I do love you both—just not the way you want me to." I looked down. "Now I feel like I led you on—even though I promise I didn't realize it wasn't going to work out until just now." I shook my head, guilt welling up inside me. I hated letting people down.

Thinking about Pryce is what made me realize throuplehood wasn't what I wanted. At least not right now.

Ben slowly nodded and then looked at his wife, who was getting downright cozy with Evan at this point. "I was afraid you'd say that." He sighed, obviously disappointed in me. "Every time we seemed to be getting close...you seemed to pull away. I thought time alone with us might win you over for good, but I guess not."

"It has nothing to do with either of you. You two are... well, you're the loveliest couple," I assured him. Then I turned toward Yvonne, whose eyes were glued to her hands clasped in her lap. With one finger, I lifted her chin toward me and gave her a soft, apologetic smile. "I really do appreciate your patience with me, your willingness to let me explore while I figured out what I wanted."

"I'm sorry it didn't work out," she said, her voice just barely above a whisper.

Their disappointment was painfully ripping through me, but I couldn't commit to them. It wouldn't be fair to any of us. I wistfully stared at the archway that led to the main part of the restaurant, wondering where Pryce was and what he was feeling right now.

I turned my attention back to the faces around the table. "Running into Pryce, it really opened my eyes. I'm still curious about what's out there, what could be waiting for me...*who* could be waiting for me. Whether it's Pryce or someone—"

"Oh, it's Pryce," Evan insisted, nodding and grinning, "don't ask me how I know, but I just do. I feel it deep in here." He patted his chest right over his heart. "And I have just the plan for getting you two back together again..."

12

PRYCE

*T*he Fantasies Fulfilled Restaurant at the top of Rainbow Castle was mind-boggling. Just when I thought I'd noticed every tiny detail, something new and breathtaking caught my eye. As an architect, I likely saw details no one else would notice. I sat in the booth for several minutes, just taking it in, not even realizing Evan was running late.

It was slightly disappointing to be waiting for my buddy to show up and not a beautiful woman. That was why I'd come to Spicetopia—to hook up and get my ex out of my mind. Instead, I'd stumbled upon the first girl I ever had feelings for, and I hadn't been able to stop thinking of her since.

I had it bad for her.

It was probably good I walked out of The Glory Hole. It was much too soon to get into another relationship,

81

right? Could I even be in a relationship with someone who was used to dating couples?

Still, I would always wonder "what if…" Not that I hadn't been wondering "what if" about Penny for two decades now already. I guess it was good practice for the rest of my life. Sigh.

"Pryce?" a soft feminine voice asked, and my head jerked up, expecting to see a server or Spicetopia staff member. But there, in all her goddess-like glory, stood Penny, resplendent in a gold sequined halter-top gown that accentuated her curvy figure and buxom breasts.

My heart leaped into my throat. "Penny, what are you doing here?" I choked out.

"Your friend Evan told me I should meet you here…" She glanced around the restaurant, lips curling up into a tentative smile. "This place is epic. Do you mind if I sit down?"

"Evan? But—how?" I stammered. I was so stunned to see her—that she was real and not a figment of my imagination—I stumbled over my words but nodded vigorously so she would grasp my meaning. I swallowed down a big gulp of water, trying to cool the flames of heat shooting through my body at her mere presence.

She climbed into the booth opposite me, her smile never faltering. "I hope you're not disappointed to see me," she began, her perfectly manicured fingers gliding over the menu.

"Well, you're a helluva lot prettier than Evan," I joked.

Her face lit up at that. "He's a really nice guy, though. I ran into him when he was looking for you at The Glory Hole—after you—"

"After I left," I finished for her, then reached out and laid my hand over hers. "As soon as I stormed out, I realized I was wrong. Well, maybe not right away, but definitely after I reflected on things a bit."

A soft, amused smile curved her full lips, and the candlelight danced in her turquoise eyes.

Taking her hand into mine and stroking my thumb over her smooth skin, I continued, "When my ex and I fought, we both had the tendency to get so mad, we walked away. One day, she walked away and never came back. I should have learned she only did it to hurt and control me. She was manipulating me and trying to force me to come crawling back to her. Yet I did the same thing to you."

"Did you want me to come crawling to you?" Her eyelashes fluttered as she searched my face for answers.

"I think I did…" I let out a deep sigh. "I felt betrayed, even though I had no right to. I didn't even give you a chance to explain."

"Betrayed how?" Her head tilted, her long fiery tresses falling gently over her smooth, rounded shoulder.

How did I explain this without sounding like an overly possessive asshole? "Because that couple you're seeing has had you—has had the pleasure of your company—for who knows how long. And I've been missing out." I chuckled softly, letting her know I was being a little playful—but there was some truth to it. I was jealous of anyone who got to spend time with this beautiful goddess sitting across from me.

She smiled, her eyes twinkling in the candlelight that flickered from the bowl of floating votives marking the space between us. "As I told you earlier today, Pryce, I never forgot you—not even after all these years. And I've always wondered what might have happened if we'd—"

"I don't think we can ever know the answer to that question," I argued. The smile faded from my lips as I turned to face the looming elephant-in-the-room question. Her answer to this one would seal our fates. "I know we just reconnected, Penny, but I have to know. Are you in love with them? This couple who brought you to Spicetopia?"

She sighed, her eyes focused on the candlelight before trailing up to meet my questioning gaze. "I was in love with the idea of being part of something, something safe, something loving, something forever. But I don't think I am in love with *them*—not the way they need me to be." Her turquoise eyes found mine, and she drilled in deep. "I want that with someone, but it's not them..."

She blinked a few times, looking at me as if she'd just batted the proverbial ball to my side of the court. Neither of us wanted to scare the other off. The tension mounted, forming a thick wall between us. I took a deep breath and decided to be brave. To lay my cards on the table.

This was Penny—my Penny—and it was now or never.

"I want that with someone too," I choked out, watching her eyelashes flutter as she processed my statement. But instead of answering, she took a sip of the wine the server had brought.

"Are you polyamorous, then?" I was struggling to understand where that left us. "And bisexual?"

Her wine glass clinked onto the table, and her eyes met mine again. "I'm bisexual, but that doesn't mean I can't commit to one person," she explained. "As for whether or not I can be or want to be monogamous—I don't know, to be honest. I haven't had a monogamous relationship since college. Is that a deal breaker?"

Was I surprised this fiery goddess I met twenty years ago grew up to be polyamorous and bisexual? Considering how precocious she was back then, how she seemed so damn comfortable in her own skin even as a teenager —no, I didn't think it was surprising at all.

All the potential scenarios were racing through my mind, just like when I was considering different design options for a building. In this case, it wasn't a physical structure I was designing but an abstract one: a relationship. A lifetime of love, happiness, and fulfillment were on the line.

My heart and head were squaring off, and as soon as the feelings bubbled up inside me, looking at her, I knew who the victor would be.

I wanted a chance with her—if polyamorous was who she was, then I would have to accept that. "It's not a deal breaker," I stated decisively. "So what does that mean for you and me?"

"I don't know, Pryce." Her gaze stabbed into mine, full of honesty and transparency. "We just reconnected, and there's so much we have to catch up on. I don't even know anything about your life, your goals, your—"

I squeezed her hand again, chuckling at how flustered she'd suddenly become. "I'm not asking you to have all that figured out right this minute."

Her auburn brows furrowed. "You're not?"

I laughed, shaking my head. "Normally, I do like to

have everything planned out—but see where that got me? My perfectly planned ten-year marriage just ended. Maybe it's like Evan is always telling me, I need to take things day by day. See where they go."

She smiled, nodding. "I'm a kindergarten teacher—taking things day by day is right up my alley. So you're not ready to—"

"Commit?" I shook my head. "Not right this second..." I took in her lovely face, her stunning features, "but ask me again tomorrow." I lifted her hand to my lips and pressed a kiss to it. "You are so beautiful, after all—even more beautiful than when we were kids."

"Is that so?" She rolled her eyes, but a playful smirk appeared on her full, luscious lips.

"That's definitely so." I nodded, enjoying the candle-light dancing in her eyes.

She straightened her shoulders, her chin lifting. "So what do you want to do now?"

I leaned forward. "How much longer are you in the Bahamas?"

"Five more days," she said, blinking. It looked as though she might be holding her breath.

I'd have to extend my trip—I really was flying by the seat of my pants now. Evan would be so proud. "Well, then, I propose we spend the next five days figuring out the next steps...and getting reacquainted with each other." Those last few words were heavily laced with innuendo.

She giggled, her lashes lowering and then rising again until her eyes met mine. "You know what? I think this restaurant is living up to its name."

AFTER DINNER, we strolled down Main Street as large crowds gathered for the nightly fireworks display in front of Rainbow Castle. I knew the evening show here was world-renowned, but I had some other fireworks in mind.

"Where are we going?" Penny asked as she looped her arm through mine.

"I have a feeling the beach will be deserted." I glanced down at her walking in step beside me and gave her a wink.

Her response was a grin. We took a stone path twinkling with tiny fairy lights that veered in the direction of Spicetopia's famous Clothing Optional Beach. I was correct—not a soul in sight. Everyone was on Main Street waiting for the fireworks—or in the dungeon or at the casino.

Moonlight painted silver streaks on the sand and the crests of the waves that rolled along the shore. I guided Penny to a soft, open patch just yards from the surf and pulled her into my arms. Our lips and tongues met like our bodies had known each other forever. And maybe they had. Maybe there were versions of Penny and Pryce who fell in love in some alternate reality that began twenty years ago, and they went on to lead a life of blissful coupledom. Now perhaps we were merging all versions together in this one very real moment in time.

"I can't believe this is actually happening," she whispered in my ear as my lips trailed down her neck, blazing a path toward her sumptuous cleavage.

As she reached down to take off her sandals, I pointed to one of the cabanas just steps from the surf. The curtains were tied up on both sides, so our view of the rolling waves would not be obstructed, and we could see out the other side toward the castle as well. Holding my hand, she followed me to it, the soft sand shifting between our toes.

"Wow, it's amazing in here," she gasped. The moonlight was just bright enough to outline a huge circular lounger topped with a thick, plush cushion. A nearby cabinet held sheets, towels and other supplies. She grabbed a sheet and quickly smoothed it over the cushion.

The roar of the crashing waves filled my ears as I pressed her down on the clean, cool sheet. I'd already ripped the gold sequined dress over her head, and my gaze raked over a breathtaking view of her nude body. The moonlight danced on her luscious curves, highlighting the contours of her full breasts and wide hips. Her soft stomach dipped in at the center, a shadow marking a slight valley I wanted to explore with my tongue.

"I want to see you too," she whispered, reaching for my linen shirt.

Balancing with my weight on my wrists and hands, I leaned close enough for her to unbutton my shirt. Her fingers deftly worked to release me from it, then I slid my shorts down before tossing them aside.

She bit her lip as she stared up at me, drinking in the sight of my broad shoulders, strong arms, and thick, muscular thighs. "Holy shit, you've sure filled out nicely since we were kids," she breathed out, sounding impressed.

I chuckled. "You are a veritable goddess," I assured her, lowering my head to press my lips against her breasts. That led to my tongue encircling her nipple, hardening it to a stiff peak as I trapped it between my teeth. She cried out as I took a little nibble of one and then the other.

I lavished her breasts with attention as her muscles tensed beneath me and her back arched. Then I remembered how sweet she tasted when I had my way with her at The Glory Hole earlier today, and I couldn't wait any longer for another sampling of her nectar. I slid down her body, trailing kisses as I went, until her mound of springy auburn curls tickled my nose.

"Pryce," she moaned, her fingers threading through my hair. "Are you sure? I still owe you from earl—"

"Shhh, I want you to come on my tongue before I finally sink deep inside you. I've been waiting twenty years, and I can probably wait a few more minutes."

When I sucked her clit between my lips, she gasped, "It's not going to take long…"

As I hummed my pleasure at her smell and taste, her hips began to writhe against my face, showing me the rhythm she craved. I wanted to give her *everything* she craved, tonight and tomorrow…and every day after. This truth crystallized as she exploded on my tongue, crying out my name in the throes of passion.

As she gradually floated back to earth, she reached out to grab me by the shoulders, commanding my attention. Her gaze pierced into mine now that our eyes had adjusted to the moonlit shore. "I want you, Pryce. I've always wanted you. Please…" She reached down and took my throbbing cock into her hand, stroking it from base to tip. "Can I?"

I bit my lip as pleasure shot through me at her touch. No sooner had I rasped out the word "yes," she guided the tip into her soaked channel. Every nerve in my body lit up with anticipation as I slowly buried myself to the hilt, encased in her tight, wet walls.

"Holy fuck…" she managed, more breath than air.

I took one deep stroke and shuddered, trying to keep the cum from rocketing out of me before I was ready. Desperately trying to hold back, I forced myself to speak, hoping it would distract me enough from ravaging her and this being over in a matter of seconds. "I can't believe you feel even better than I've been imagining all these years…"

"It doesn't seem possible, does it?" She reached out to stroke her fingertips down my stubble, moaning when the roughness grated against her soft skin. "Please…please make love to me, Pryce."

Speechless from the feel of her pussy clenching around me, I began to thrust slowly. Her thick legs wrapped around my hips, urging me on. My balls ached for release as they slapped against her, and her increasingly wild moans did nothing to help me maintain a reasonable pace.

"Oh, god, Pryce, I'm gonna come," the words rushed out, and mere seconds later, her walls spasmed, milking me in a rhythm that was impossible to stroke through without losing my battle.

And just like that, an orgasm twenty years in the

making erupted from me, my seed shooting deep inside her as exquisite pleasure shattered my soul. Her arms tightened around me as we both rode out our climaxes, sealed together.

Perhaps our fates were sealed together too.

And with that thought, fireworks erupted in the distance. We both turned toward the castle to witness bursts of gold, silver, green, purple and red raining down over the rainbow spires. As her lips found mine again, I had the distinct feeling we wouldn't need five whole days to figure out our next steps. It seemed like these last five minutes were all we needed.

Penny was destined to be mine that first time I saw her at Sweetopia twenty years ago. And if the way her body melted into mine was any indication, she knew it too.

THE END

Make sure to read the whole Spicetopia series at your favorite retailer!

https://books2read.com/Spicetopia1

See all my books here: books2read.com/PhoebeAlexander

Join my newsletter here:
Bit.ly/PhoebeAlexanderNews

AUTHOR'S NOTE

*O*ne thing you may not know me is that I'm one of those annoying Disney adults. It's not really about the movies or characters for me as much as the parks. (Though I do have my favorite characters, which happen to be Ariel and Belle, for obvious reasons!) I appreciate the attention to detail and story in the parks—as a writer, how could I not? And the logistics are absolutely mind-boggling to me. I've been to Disney World many, many times, and my family considers me a professional when it comes to planning trips and navigating the parks. I would be lying if I claimed my love and knowledge of those parks didn't contribute to this series.

In any case, the idea for this story was borne out of a post I read in a group for Disney World afficionados. A woman posted looking for the mom of an eight-year-old girl named Ellie. The two families were staying at the same resort. The woman's son, Jack, had given Ellie a heart gem from his souvenir set and claimed she was the girl he was going to marry someday. Jack's mom was wondering whether she needed to start saving now for Jack and Ellie's Disney wedding.

The more I thought about it, the more the idea grew on me to write a version of this for Sweetopia/Spicetopia. And so here we are...

ABOUT THE AUTHOR

USA Today Bestselling Author Phoebe Alexander writes sexpositive, bodypositive erotic romance and believes that real, relatable characters can have even steamier sex than billionaires, rock stars, and the young and lithe-bodied. She also advocates for ethical non-monogamy through her writing.

Phoebe lives on the US East Coast with her husband and multiple fur babies, and is the mother of three adult sons. When she's not writing, she works as an editor and consultant for indie authors. She also owns the 6000-member Indie Author Support group on Facebook. Her sexual fantasies have all been fulfilled, and now her single greatest fantasy is just having some damn free time.

Newsletter: http://www.phoebe-alexander.com
Facebook Group: http://www.facebook.com/groups/PhoebesAngels
Instagram: http://www.instagram.com/authorphoebealexander
BookBub: http://www.bookbub.com/authors/phoebe-alexander

ALSO BY PHOEBE ALEXANDER

Mountains Trilogy

Mountains Wanted

Mountains Climbed

Mountains Loved

Christmas in the Mountains

The Navigator

The Explorer

The Adventurer

Mountains Transcended

Eastern Shore Swingers Series

Fisher of Men

The Catch

Siren Call

Sailors Knot

Turning the Tide

Spicetopia Series

Sugar & Spice

Virtue & Vice

Fire & Ice

Naughty & Nice

Dares & Dice

Loyalty & Lies

Penny & Pryce

Spice Up Our Marriage Series

Project Paradise

Rule Breaker

The Playground

Keeping Secrets

The Ruse

Alpha Bet Guys Series

A Hole

The Big O

Need the D

Hard F

Ride the C

Standalones

Authority Issues

Clean Grammar for Dirty Minds

Made in the USA
Middletown, DE
08 September 2023

38201891R00061